Dog Days for Dudley

by Barbara Moe

illustrated by Sylvie Wickstrom

Bradbury Press · New York

Maxwell Macmillan Canada • Toronto
Maxwell Macmillan International
New York • Oxford • Singapore • Sydney

Bradbury Press
Macmillan Publishing Company
866 Third Avenue
New York, NY 10022

Maxwell Macmillan Canada, Inc.
1200 Eglinton Avenue East
Suite 200
Don Mills, Ontario M3C 3N1

Macmillan Publishing Company is part of the Maxwell Communication
Group of Companies.

First edition
Printed and bound in Singapore
10 9 8 7 6 5 4 3 2 1

The text of this book is set in 14-point Clearface.
The illustrations are rendered in watercolor and ink.
Library of Congress Cataloging-in-Publication Data
Moe, Barbara A.
    Dog days for Dudley / by Barbara Moe ; illustrated by Sylvie Wickstrom.
        p.   cm.
    Summary: Seven-year-old Dudley tries to convince his father to get him a puppy.
    ISBN: 0-02-767260-3
    [1. Dogs—Fiction.] I. Wickstrom, Sylvie, ill. II. Title.
PZ7.M718Do   1994
[E]—dc20   92-5167

For Chris

—BM

To Thor

—SW

Contents

Dog Days for Dudley

1

Dudley Wants a Dog

Dudley Wolf glanced out the classroom window. A small boy chased a dog through a pile of fall leaves.

Every time Dudley saw a dog, he thought one thing: That's what I want. A dog.

Dudley sighed. Then he began writing his book.

"Hey," said Abigail Chin. Abigail always said "hey." She was the prettiest girl in Ms. Miller's second grade. "You have your nose on your paper, Dudley."

Dudley didn't look up. Whenever Abigail talked to him, his face got hot. He didn't want Abigail to see his red-hot face.

Dudley kept writing. He wasn't a good speller, but he drew nice pictures. Last year he *only* drew pictures. He didn't get his book published because his book didn't have any words.

Last year Ms. Skinner was Dudley's teacher. She said a book without words wasn't a book. Dudley had shown Ms. Skinner three library books with no words. She still didn't change her mind.

This year Dudley's book would have lots of words. He was calling it *Dudley Wants a Dog*.

Writing a book was hard work. Dudley had to erase a lot. Write, erase. Write, erase. Dudley bent over his paper and wrote:

> *Dudley wanted a puppy very much.*
> *He was an only child.*
> *Sometimes he got lonely.*

Dudley drew a picture to go with the words. He put a red ribbon on his new puppy. The puppy's head stuck out of a box.

Abigail Chin looked at Dudley's picture. "Hey, you're a real artist."

"Thanks," said Dudley.

Ms. Miller looked over Dudley's shoulder. "Good start, young man."

Dudley sat up straighter. Tia Bostwick peeked over his other shoulder. "Yikes," she said. "Look at all that erasing. And you're only on page one!"

Dudley sank down in his seat. This time it was Tia who made his face get hot. Only now it was *mad*-hot.

"I'm almost finished with *my* book," said Tia. "At my old school I wrote five books."

Blah, blah, thought Dudley. Tia was always talking about her old school. She thought she was so smart.

Dudley erased the last sentence. He didn't want anyone to know he got lonely sometimes. His eraser made a hole in his paper.

He got another piece of paper out of his notebook and wrote a different sentence.

Dudley's dad thought puppies were too much trouble.

Dudley's new friend, Jason Jackson, walked by. He bumped Dudley's elbow. "Sorry, pal," he said.

"No problem," said Dudley.

Jason leaned over. "You're working hard."

"True," Dudley answered. He wished he were Jason. Jason had a little brother, three dogs, two cats, a bird, and a guinea pig. Jason probably never got lonely.

Dudley wrote another sentence.

His dad thought Dudley wouldn't take
care of a puppy.

He stopped writing. He had to come up for air.
He went to sharpen his pencil.

Abigail Chin was sharpening her pencil, too.
"Hey, Dudley, look at your nose. You have a pencil-
lead nose. What do you think of that?"

Dudley stared at her. Was she crazy? How did
she expect him to look at his own nose? Besides,
he didn't care what Abigail thought. He wanted

to think about getting a puppy. Maybe if he showed his book to his father, his dad would let him get one.

Dudley went back to his desk and read his story so far.

Dudley wanted a puppy very much.
He was an only child.
Dudley's dad thought puppies were
too much trouble.
His dad thought Dudley wouldn't take
care of a puppy.

Then Dudley wrote:

But he would.

Two days later Dudley finished his rough draft. Ms. Miller told him to take *Dudley Wants a Dog* to the publishing house in room 201. Miss Travis opened up the publishing house every Wednesday afternoon. Miss Travis was a retired librarian. She and the teachers picked the smartest sixth graders to be editors.

Walter Prince was Dudley's editor. Dudley admired Walter, the student-council president. Walter was nice and also brainy. He corrected Dudley's misspelled words and rearranged some of the sentences.

"This is quite a book," said Walter. "Did you know dogs are the fifth most intelligent animals?"

"How do you know that?" Dudley asked.

"I read encyclopedias in my spare time," said Walter.

On Friday Dudley finished his final copy: *Dudley Wants a Dog* by Dudley Wolf, author and illustrator. He took his book home and read the whole thing to his mother. "Like it?" he asked.

His mother gave him a hug. "My little author," she said. "I love your book, and I love you."

"I love you, too," Dudley said. "Dad, too, but I'd love him even more if he let me have a puppy. When you were a kid, did you ever want a dog?"

"Would you like to hear a secret?" asked his mother.

"Shoot," said Dudley.

"I wouldn't mind having a puppy. I always had a dog when I was your age, but your dad never did. And he doesn't think we need one now."

"I know," Dudley said.

"I guess your father only likes animals at a distance," said Dudley's mother.

Dudley wanted to show the book to his father, but Mr. Wolf hadn't come home from work yet. Dudley left his book on the piano bench.

When his father came home, Dudley made a dash for his book. "You'll love this, Dad."

Mr. Wolf read the whole thing out loud. "Not bad, kiddo." He nodded. "Nice work."

Dudley took a deep breath. "So do you think I could have a puppy?"

Mr. Wolf ran a hand through his hair. "A *puppy?* I'm too old for a puppy."

"But Dad," said Dudley, "*I'm* the one who wants a puppy. I'll take care of it."

"A puppy?" said Dudley's dad again. "Are you sure? Puppies are a lot of work. You have to feed them, brush them, walk them, and clean up after them. We might even have to build a doghouse."

"That would be fun," said Dudley.

"I don't have time," said his father. "I have to raise funds for the zoo." Dudley's father was an important man at the zoo. He was Chairman of the Board. His father patted his chest. "How I love the roar of the lion and the bark of the seal. I'd like for us to walk over there after dinner and see the baby hippopotamus. Or we could watch the sea lions swim."

"But Dad," Dudley argued, "I can't *pet* a sea lion. I can't hold the baby hippo in my lap."

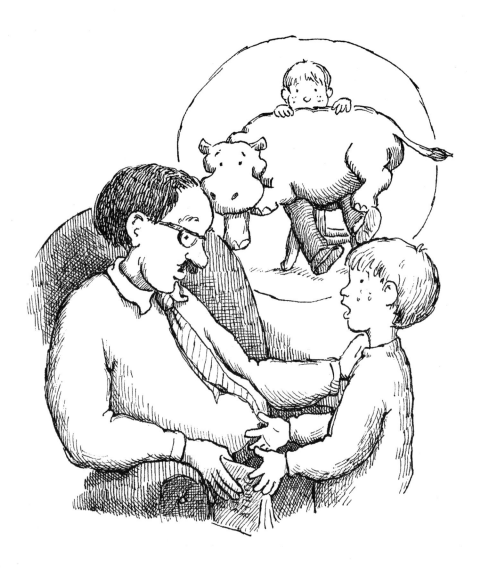

His father laughed. "I know you'd rather go to the zoo with your friends. By the way, your teacher called today. She wanted me to arrange a trip for your class."

His father had changed the subject. He didn't seem ready for a puppy. Dudley didn't want to make him mad or hurt his feelings. But he didn't want to go to the zoo with his father. He didn't want to go to the zoo with his class or with his friends. He didn't want to go there at all. He was tired of it. He'd spent half his life at the zoo.

"Dad," Dudley said, "maybe we could go together some other time. How about Father's Day?"

"No problem," said his dad.

After dinner Dudley went to the family room. He got some paper and a pencil. He found the *D* encyclopedia in the bookcase. He took it to his front porch and sat down on the top step.

He looked at the colored pictures of dogs. Soon he was *drawing* pictures of dogs. First he drew a chow chow. Then he drew a bulldog. Last he drew a poodle.

By this time his hand was tired. He looked up. Abigail Chin was walking down the street. Dudley held the *D* encyclopedia in front of his face.

Suddenly Abigail was leaning over it. "Hey, whatcha doing?"

"Reading about dogs," said Dudley.

"It doesn't look to me like you're reading." Abigail inspected his pictures. "It looks to me like you're drawing."

"You're right," said Dudley. "I ended up drawing. But I started out reading—about dogs."

"Why?" Abigail asked. "Are you getting one?"

"I'd like to, but my dad won't let me. I don't think he wants to build a doghouse."

"You could show him you mean business," said Abigail. "*You* could build a doghouse."

"I guess I could," said Dudley. "I hadn't thought of that. Thanks."

"Sure," said Abigail. "Bye."

Dudley gathered up his papers and went inside. "Mom, where's Dad?" he asked.

"He's down in the workshop fixing a lamp," his mother answered.

Dudley went downstairs. "Hey, Dad, could I use some of your old wood scraps?"

"Of course," said his dad. "What are you going to make?"

"A doghouse," said Dudley. "Just in case."

"Are you sure you know how?" asked Mr. Wolf.

"I can try." Dudley went to work hammering and nailing. *Hammer, hammer.* He hit his finger.

"Ouch!" said Dudley. Tears came to his eyes, but he didn't cry. He didn't want his dad to think he was a baby, someone who couldn't take care of a puppy.

Finally he hammered the last nail. He stood back and admired his work. "How's this, Dad?"

"Not bad," said his father. "It looks more like a box."

"It *is* a box," said Dudley. "A puppy box." He sucked on his sore finger and wished for a dog.

2

Zoo Day

*O*n Monday Ms. Miller had a surprise for her second graders. Not for Dudley. He already knew the plan. He prayed Ms. Miller wouldn't say anything about his father and embarrass him.

"On Wednesday," said Ms. Miller, "we are going to the zoo. Dudley's father has so kindly arranged a trip for us."

Dudley groaned—under his breath.

"Please ask your parents to sign these permission slips," said Ms. Miller. "Anyone without a signed permission slip will have to spend the morning with the first graders."

Dudley rubbed his head. He didn't want to go to the zoo, but he didn't want to spend even half a day with the little kids.

Jason sat next to Dudley. As soon as Ms. Miller said "zoo," Jason started drumming on his desk. "Polar bears, sea lions, monkeys," he said. He turned to Dudley. "I heard the zoo has a baby hippo. Have you seen it?"

"Jason Jackson is not listening," said Ms. Miller. "Jason, could I please have your ears?"

Jason put his hands on the sides of his head. He tried to pull off his ears. Some of the kids laughed.

Ms. Miller looked over Jason's head and talked to the class. "We are going to learn which animals are in danger of becoming extinct."

"Does *extinct* mean they smell bad?" Jason sat tall in his seat.

Everyone laughed, except Ms. Miller. She frowned at Jason. "Does anyone know what *extinct* means?"

Dudley raised his hand.

"Yes, Dudley."

"Extinct is when animals die out. People have invaded their lands."

"Correct," said Ms. Miller. "And now it's up to people to help the animals survive."

That night for dinner the Wolf family had chicken stir-fry. Dudley didn't want to eat chicken. "I don't want chickens to become extinct."

"No danger," said his father. "When I was a boy your age, we raised chickens."

"I don't want to raise chickens," said Dudley. "I want a puppy."

Mr. Wolf glanced at Mrs. Wolf. "Just as raising chickens requires work, so does caring for a puppy." He took another bite of chicken stir-fry.

By Wednesday everyone in Ms. Miller's class had brought back a signed permission slip. "Before we go to the zoo, everyone must pick a buddy." Ms. Miller propped a pencil on top of her ear. "We have twenty-seven class members and two parent volunteers. That's twenty-nine, an odd number. I will be the leftover person's buddy."

"The odd person," said Jason.

"That's you!" Tia Bostwick pointed at Jason and laughed. "You're an odd person, Jason."

Jason frowned, but Dudley smiled at him.

Sometimes the other kids teased Jason because he had animal hairs on his jeans. Dudley wished *he* had dog hairs on *his* jeans.

"Please quiet down, people," said Ms. Miller. "Let's get on with buddy picking."

Dudley picked Jason.

"Thanks, Dud," said Jason. "I was afraid I'd be the oddball."

A few seconds later Abigail Chin tapped Dudley's arm. "Want to be my buddy?"

"Oh, wow! I mean, sure. But I already picked Jason."

Abigail wrinkled up her nose and put her hands on her hips. "It looks like I'm the leftover."

"That's fine, Abigail," said Ms. Miller. "You will be my buddy. Now, class, let's proceed to the bus."

Dudley and Jason walked through the hall together. Dudley was glad to be Jason's buddy. He admired the way Jason joked around. Jason made other people laugh.

"You know what?" Jason asked.

"What?" said Dudley.

"The other day when we were making books, I saw your puppy pictures." Jason gave Dudley his thumbs-up sign. "Would you like a puppy? I found

this mutt a week ago in my yard. We put an ad in the paper. Nobody wanted him."

"Wow," said Dudley. His heart beat faster. "Can't you keep him?"

Jason shook his head. "My parents said we already have enough animals."

"You mean you have to *give* him away?"

"Yep," Jason said.

"I can't have a puppy," said Dudley. "My dad only likes zoo animals."

"Well," said Jason, "I thought I'd give you first chance. Maybe someone else in our class would like him. My mom wants me to bring him to show-and-tell tomorrow."

The bus ride took only a few minutes. On the way Dudley kept thinking about Jason's puppy and imagining what he looked like.

At the zoo entrance Ms. Miller and the class gathered for a meeting. "You must each take care of your buddy," she said. "I told a friend of mine we would be here today. She's a photographer for the *Granite City Gazette*."

31

"Should we smile for the camera?" Jason asked.

"No," said Ms. Miller. "She might take some-one's picture, but I want you to go about your business as if she wasn't there." Ms. Miller took Abigail's hand. "We will now proceed to the bird house."

Dudley and Jason didn't hold hands. They stayed together, though. "My dad's trying to raise money for a new sprinkler system in this bird house," said Dudley. "I don't like the bird house. I'm al-ways worried that one of the birds flying around in there will—you know—"

Jason put his hand on his head. "That's why I wore my baseball cap."

In the bird house they saw a lady with a big camera. Dudley tried not to look at her. Then he felt a drip on his head. "Uh-oh," he said, "it happened."

At the same time, a camera flashed. Dudley barely noticed. He was too busy touching his head. "Check my hair, buddy," he said. "I feel something wet up there."

Jason checked. "Don't worry. It's just water from the sprinklers."

"Whew," Dudley said. "I *was* worried."

After they went through the bird house, Jason asked, "Can we go see the polar bears, sea lions, and monkeys?"

"We won't have time to see everything this morning," said Ms. Miller. "We'll come back some other time. Today we'll concentrate on the animals in danger of becoming extinct."

"Where are we going?' asked Sam.

"To the pachyderm house," said Ms. Miller. "I want you to see the baby hippopotamus. Her name is Louise."

On the way to the pachyderm house, some of the kids started talking. "What kind of zoo animal would you like to have in your backyard?" Jason asked.

"I'd take an elephant," said Tia. "I have a huge backyard."

"I'd like to dig a pool and have a sea lion," said Clifton.

"I want a peacock," said Abigail. "I like to watch them strut their stuff." She turned to Dudley.

"What kind of animal do you want?"

"I want a puppy," said Dudley.

Everyone laughed.

At the pachyderm house they saw Baby Louise.
She was three months old and weighed about three
hundred pounds.

Before they left the zoo, they saw animals in danger of becoming extinct—the black rhinoceros, the horned oryx, the wattled crane, and the reindeer.

Finally Ms. Miller told them it was time to leave. "Back to school, class."

On the way to the bus, Jason talked about the zoo animals they'd seen. Dudley thought about dogs. "I can't wait until show-and-tell tomorrow," he said to Jason. "Do you think I could hold your puppy?"

3

Mutt Comes to Class

On Thursday Ms. Miller introduced Jason's mother. "Ladies and gentlemen, we have two guests, Mrs. Jackson and her puppy. Please give them your attention."

Jason's mother smiled at the class. She held up the puppy. "He's an Australian shepherd mix, and we call him Mutt," she said. "We hope the person who keeps him will give him a real name."

Mutt had a tan coat with a white fur shield on his chest. He had floppy ears, white-tipped paws, and a wiggly black nose. He nibbled on Mrs. Jackson's hand.

"I'd like to have him," said Clifton. "I'd call him Amy."

"Amy?" asked Jason's mom. "Why would you pick a girl's name for this little pooch?"

"Because my sister's name is Amy," Clifton answered. "Mutt has short hair just like my sister."

"I think I should get him," said Tia. "I'd name him Chocolate."

"Chocolate?" said Mrs. Jackson. "Even though Mutt is a caramel-colored puppy?"

"Tia likes chocolate," said Jason.

"I'd call him Fluff," said Abigail.

"Why is that?" asked Jason's mother.

"Because he's fluffy," said Abigail.

"Fluff sounds like a cat's name," said Sam.

Dudley squirmed. He wanted to suggest a name, but he didn't. He knew his dad wouldn't let him have Mutt.

"I think that's enough on names," said Ms. Miller. "Jason's mother and I have decided something. I can see that several of you would like this puppy for your very own."

Heads nodded.

Ms. Miller went on. "I have prepared a notice for you to take to your parents. The notice says you and your parents agree to provide a loving home for Mutt."

"That'll be easy," said Robert.

Clifton nodded. "I can do it."

"Does anyone know about caring for puppies?" asked Jason's mom.

"Don't let them eat chocolate-covered cherries," said Tia. "Chocolate candy makes them sick."

"Tia is right," said Ms. Miller. "Too much chocolate isn't good for puppies or for humans."

Sam held his hand in the air.

"Sam?"

"I let my puppy sleep in my room the first week. She got used to me that way."

"We put our puppy in my sister's old playpen at night," said Kendra.

Jason's mother nodded. "Interesting ideas."

"Anything else?" asked Ms. Miller.

"You have to take them outside after they eat," said Robert. "They'll get housebroken that way. Then you have to praise them."

"Excellent," said Ms. Miller. "Praise works well for dogs."

Abigail raised her hand. "Don't let them chew electric wires. They could get electrocoated."

"Electro*cut*ed," said Ms. Miller. She scratched Mutt behind his ear. "I know everyone would like to hold this sweet puppy," she said. "But we don't have much more time this morning. I'm going to ask Jason to pick *one* puppy holder."

Suddenly Jason was very popular. A dozen hands shot into the air. "Jason," everyone yelled. "Remember me? I'm your best friend."

Jason nodded at Dudley. "This may be your only chance to hold Mutt." Jason gave him the puppy. Mutt nibbled on Dudley's thumb. Then he cuddled into Dudley's lap and closed his eyes.

Everyone in the room got quiet. Then other kids

40

began to shake their hands in the air and beg to hold Mutt. But Jason's mother had to leave.

After Mrs. Jackson left, Ms. Miller pulled a newspaper clipping from her desk drawer. "Did any of you see the *Gazette* this morning?" She held up a picture. It showed Dudley and Jason in the tropical bird forest. Dudley stared up at the trees with a wide-eyed look. He had his hand on his head. Jason tugged on the visor of his baseball cap. The headline said ZOO SEEKS FUNDS FOR BIRD HOUSE SPRINKLER.

"Wow, Dud," said Abigail, "you're in the paper. You're famous."

"If I'm famous," Dudley said, "then Jason must be famous, too. He's in the same picture."

Jason looked at his shoes. "It was nothing." He looked up. "But I don't mind being a little bit famous."

Dudley smiled at his friend. But Dudley didn't want to be famous. He wanted a puppy, the puppy he had just held.

That night at dinner he asked his dad about the puppy. "All you have to do is sign a teensy-weensy notice," Dudley begged.

Dudley's mother leaned her head on her hand and looked at Dudley's dad. "What do you think, hon? I wouldn't mind."

"Well," said Dudley's dad, "maybe we can talk about it later."

He took a bite of lettuce. *Crunch, crunch.* How could he *eat* at a time like this? thought Dudley.

The next day no one brought back a puppy notice.

"I want him, but we already have two dogs,"

said Sam. "My parents said no."

"My mom said I'd have to buy the dog food out of my allowance," said Clifton Brown. "I only get two dollars a week."

"We live in a no-pet apartment building," said Robert. "I thought I could get our landlady to change her mind. She said no dice."

Dudley picked some imaginary dog hairs off his jeans. What would happen to Mutt? He pictured Mutt in an alley, raiding garbage cans. People might scream at him or throw rocks. In a way, though, Dudley was glad no one had brought back a notice. If *he* couldn't have Mutt, he didn't want anyone else to have him.

After lunch Tia Bostwick marched up to Ms. Miller. She handed her a piece of folded paper.

"What is it, Tia?" Ms. Miller read the note. Her eyebrows wrinkled like two furry caterpillars. "Did your mother sign this?"

Tia nodded.

"Thank you, Tia. We'll talk later." Ms. Miller put the note in her top desk drawer.

Dudley felt a hollow feeling in his stomach. His eyes stung, but he told himself not to cry. As much as he hated to admit the fact, Mutt would probably be better off at Tia's than with no home at all. Still, he felt sad.

Right after school Jason had to leave for the dentist. He punched Dudley in the arm. "Bad luck," he said. "That Tia gets Mutt, I mean."

"I know," Dudley said. He went home, headed straight for his room, and drew dog pictures till dinnertime. He couldn't get Mutt out of his head.

Dudley didn't eat much for dinner.

"Are you sick?" asked his mom.

"Just a little," Dudley said.

46

Someone knocked on the door. He went to answer it. Jason stood outside, with Mutt in his arms.

"Hi, Jason," said Dudley. "Hi, Mutt. What are you doing here? I thought you'd be taking Mutt to Tia's tonight."

Mutt nibbled on Jason's arm. "Tia's in big trouble," Jason said.

"She is?" asked Dudley. "How come?"

"You know the notice Ms. Miller gave us?"

Dudley nodded.

"Tia's mother didn't sign it," Jason said. "Tia did. She forged her mom's name. Ms. Miller suspected it right away, but she didn't want to embarrass Tia."

"How did Ms. Miller know?" asked Dudley.

Jason smiled. "Tia signed the note 'Tia's mother.'"

"Poor Tia," Dudley said. She wasn't so smart after all. In the future, Dudley decided, he would try to be nicer to her.

Jason held out Mutt. "Want to hold him?"

"Sure!" Dudley held out his arms. Mutt licked his face, then settled down. Dudley felt like the King of the World. He couldn't imagine any other place he'd rather be right now.

Jason pulled a crumpled piece of newspaper out of his pocket. He held up the clipping with the picture of himself and Dudley in the bird house. "I brought this to show your father. Did he see it yet?"

"I don't know." Dudley rubbed Mutt's soft fur. "He didn't mention it."

"Didn't you *ask* him?"

"I forgot," said Dudley. "I was too busy thinking about Mutt."

"Go get your dad," said Jason. "Here. I'll take Mutt. We'll wait outside."

Dudley hated to part with Mutt, but he handed him to Jason and went inside to get his dad.

When they returned, Dudley introduced his friend. "Dad, this is Jason, my friend from school."

"Hi, Jason," said Mr. Wolf. "How's it going?"

"Hello, Mr. Wolf." Jason held out the clipping. "Did you see your son in the *Gazette?*"

"We get the *Post,*" said Mr. Wolf. "But one of my coworkers brought me the picture. You're in there too, Jason. It's good."

"Thanks," said Jason. "I don't mind being famous."

Mr. Wolf looked at Mutt. "That's a nice puppy you have."

"I can't keep it, though," said Jason. "My parents are old meanies."

The boys looked at each other and laughed.

Mr. Wolf gave Mutt a pat.

"Besides," Jason added, "we already have three dogs, two cats, one bird, and a guinea pig."

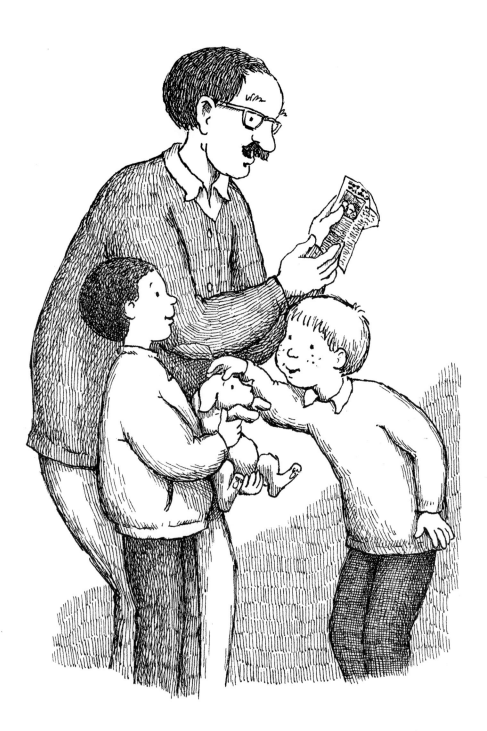

"How about us, Dad? Couldn't we have Mutt?" Dudley begged.

Dudley's father shook his head. "Such a large puppy. If only he were a bit smaller."

"Size doesn't matter, Dad. I can handle him. I promise to take good care of him."

Jason glanced up at Dudley's father. "You could make him sign a contract."

Mr. Wolf raised his eyebrows. "A contract?"

"Something like this," said Jason. " 'I, Dudley, promise to take good care of this puppy. I will feed him, give him fresh water, play with him, and clean up his messes every day.' Something like that."

"Perfect," said Dudley. "Please, Dad?"

4

A Puppy for Dudley?

*D*udley got down on his knees. He folded his hands and looked up at his father.

"Please get up, Dudley," said Mr. Wolf. "You look funny down there." He crossed his arms on his chest. "Don't you realize there is much to consider when getting a puppy? For example, where would he sleep?"

Dudley stood up. "Sometimes puppies sleep in a playpen." He glanced over at Mutt.

"We don't have a playpen," said his father.

"A box would work," Dudley mumbled. "The box I built would be nice. He could sleep in my room at night."

"I'm happy with my zoo animals," said Mr. Wolf. "I can't understand why a whole zoo full of animals less than a mile away isn't enough for you." He winked at Jason.

"What's so great about the zoo?" Dudley asked.

"It's important to give city kids a chance to see wild animals up close," said Jason.

"Right," said Mr. Wolf. "We also try to keep certain animals from becoming extinct."

"From dying out," Jason said. "That's what we're studying in school. Humans have invaded a lot of the animals' lands."

"I've known that for about five years," said Dudley.

Just then the phone rang. Dudley's mom stuck her head out the door. "It's for you, Winthrop."

Dudley's dad went inside.

While he was gone the boys played with Mutt. Jason pulled a tennis ball out of his back pocket. Mutt tried to chew up the ball.

Suddenly Dudley's father ran out. *"Whoo!"* he shouted.

"What happened?" asked Jason.

"One of my board members called," said Mr. Wolf.

"What for?" Dudley asked.

"She had a good idea about how we can raise funds for the bird house sprinkler system," said Mr. Wolf.

"Excellent," said Jason. "Like what?"

"She saw your pictures and the story in the paper," Dudley's dad went on. "She suggested we could raise funds by selling bird-beak baseball caps."

"You mean like *my* baseball cap?" Jason asked.

"Yes," said Mr. Wolf. "Caps similar to the one you wore in the picture."

"Sounds great," said Dudley.

His dad nodded. "You boys deserve a reward. What would you like?"

"A puppy," said Dudley.

Dudley's father rubbed his chin. Then he

scooped up Mutt. "You mean *this* puppy?"

Dudley reached over and scratched Mutt's head. "His name is Mutt."

Mr. Wolf stared at Jason. "Does Mutt chew up slippers and whine all night for his mother?"

"Sometimes," Jason said. "We gave him an old slipper to chew on. We put warm water in a jar and wrapped a soft blanket around it. The warm bottle feels like his mother."

"Did you put a clock in his box?" asked Mr. Wolf.

Dudley frowned. "What for, Dad?"

"A clock sounds like the mother's heartbeat," Jason answered. "We tried that, too."

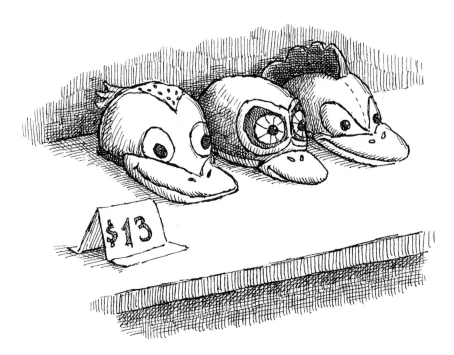

Mr. Wolf sat down on the porch step and looked at Jason. "If we don't like him, may we return him to you?"

"No, sir. You have to keep him," Jason said. "I know you'll like him. I do. And if you *do* like Mutt, that will be enough reward for me."

Mutt settled into Mr. Wolf's lap and chewed on his finger.

"Don't be an old meanie, Mr. Wolf." Jason grinned.

Mr. Wolf rubbed Mutt's back. Finally he smiled, too. "Okay, Dudley, you may have Mutt. We'll even make a contract. *If* it's all right with your mother."

"It is," Dudley answered. "She already said so."

"We'll have to think of a better name," said Mr. Wolf.

"Let's call him Nibbles," said Dudley. He couldn't stop smiling. He smiled at Jason and at his father. Then he smiled at Nibbles.

"You'll have to learn how to take care of this dog." Dudley's father put Nibbles into his arms.

"Don't worry," said Dudley. Nibbles put his head against Dudley's arm and closed his eyes.

Jason scratched Nibbles behind his ear. "I'll help teach Dudley how to take care of you."

"I'm ready to learn,"said Dudley. "But no one has to teach me to *love* Nibbles. I know how to do that already."

Just then the telephone rang again. Dudley's mother answered it. "For you, Dudley," she called.

"It's Abigail." She came to the door. "Who *is* Abigail?"

"A girl in our class." Dudley took the receiver and balanced Nibbles in the crook of his arm.

"Hi, Dudley," said Abigail's voice.

"Hi, Abigail. What's happening?"

"Jason bet me you'd get to keep Mutt. Did he win our bet?"

"You bet," said Dudley.

They both laughed.

"I was wondering if I could come over and play with him sometime," said Abigail.

Dudley grinned. "Sure! His name is Nibbles now."